10/17

P9-DMB-008

(a birthday something)
for neal —J.F.

To all children on their birthdays
—C.R.

Text copyright © 2017 by Julie Fogliano

Illustrations copyright © 2017 by Christian Robinson

A Neal Porter Book

Published by Roaring Brook Press

Roaring Brook Press is a division of

Holtzbrinck Publishing Holdings Limited Partnership

175 Fifth Avenue, New York, New York 10010

the art for this book was made using acrylic paint and collage techniques

mackids.com

All rights reserved

Library of Congress Cataloging-in-Publication Data

Names: Fogliano, Julie, author. | Robinson, Christian, illustrator.

Title: When's my birthday? / Julie Fogliano ; illustrated by Christian
Robinson.

Other titles: When is my birthday?

Description: First edition. | New York : Roaring Brook Press, 2017. |
"A Neal Porter book." | Summary: Children excitedly discuss the
details of their upcoming birthdays.

Identifiers: LCCN 2016047514 | ISBN 9781626722934 (hardcover)

Subjects: | CYAC: Birthdays—Fiction.

Classification: LCC PZ7.F6763 Wh 2017 | DDC [E]—dc23

LC record available at https://lccn.loc.gov/2016047514

Our books may be purchased in bulk for promotional, educational,
or business use. Please contact your local bookseller or the Macmillan
Corporate and Premium Sales Department at (800) 221-7945 ext. 5442
or by e-mail at MacmillanSpecialMarkets@macmillan.com.

First edition 2017

Book design by Kristie Radwilowicz

Printed in China by Toppan Leefung Printing Ltd.,
Dongguan City, Guangdong Province

1   3   5   7   9   10   8   6   4   2

when's
my
birthday?

East Bridgewater Public Library
32 Union Street
East Bridgewater, MA 02333

Julie
Fogliano

Christian
Robinson

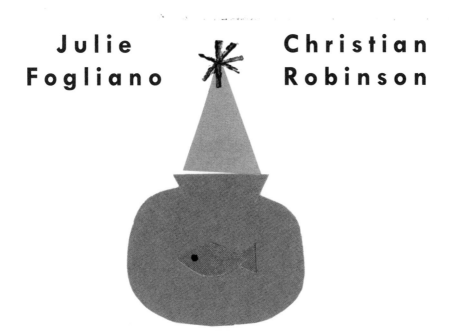

A NEAL PORTER BOOK
ROARING BROOK PRESS
NEW YORK

when's my birthday?
where's my birthday?
how many days until
my birthday?

will my birthday be on tuesday?
will my birthday be tomorrow?
will my birthday be in winter?

will my birthday be in spring?

will my birthday have some singing?
will we sing so happy happy?
will we dance around and round?
will we jump and jump and jump?

when's my birthday?
where's my birthday?
how many days until
my birthday?

i'd like a pony
for my birthday
and a necklace
for my birthday.

i'd like a
chicken for
my birthday.

i'd like a ball
to bounce
and bounce.

i'd like a big cake on my birthday
with lots of chocolate on my birthday
and lots of candles on my birthday
1, 2, 3, 4, 5, and 6!

i'd like some wishes on my birthday.
i'd like some kisses on my birthday.
i'd like some berries on my birthday
and tiny sandwiches with soup.

and you're invited
to my birthday.

and she's invited
to my birthday.

and he's invited
to my birthday.

and you and
you and you.

and you can wear your fancy dresses
or you can wear your fuzzy slippers
or you can wear a hat with feathers
or a helmet with a cape.

if it ever is my birthday . . .
will it never be my birthday?
is it almost happy birthday?
happy happy day to me!

when's my birthday?
where's my birthday?
how many days until
my birthday?

In the morning it's my birthday!

I'm not sleeping till my birthday.

I'm just waiting till my birthday.

I'm just yawning till my birthday.

I'm just dreaming of my bluuuurfday.

Happy snore and snore to me!

it's the daytime!
here's my birthday!
happy happy!
hee! hee! hee!
time for cakey
wakey wakey

happy happy day to me!

When's Your Birthday?

January 1 2 3 4

February

March 8 9 10

April

May 14 15

June

July

August 19 20 21

September

October 24 25

November

December 29 30 31

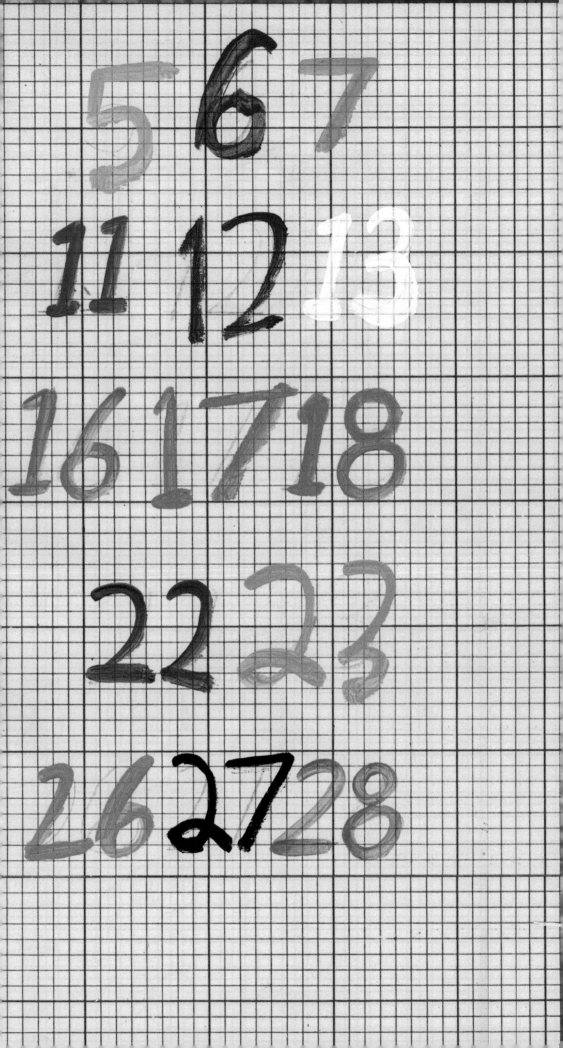